BACK TO BASICS

The Back to Basics series was devised and produced by McRae Books Srl, Borgo S. Croce, 8, Florence (Italy)

Publishers: Anne McRae and Marco Nardi
Text: Loredana Agosta, Anne McRae
Main Illustrations: Fiammetta Dogi
Other illustrations: Antonella Pastorelli, Studio Stalio (Alessandro Cantucci, Fabiano Fabbrucci, Margherita Salvadori)
Design: Marco Nardi
Layout: Rebecca Milner
Color separations: Fotolito Toscana, Firenze

Library of Congress Cataloging-in-Publication Data

McRae, Anne.
  Mammals / by Anne McRae and Loredana Agosta.
    p. cm. -- (Back to basics)
  Includes index.
  ISBN 978-8860980472 (alk. paper)
  1. Mammals--Juvenile literature. I. Agosta, Loredana.
II. Title.
  QL706.2.M37 2007
  599--dc22
                                    2007007817

Printed and bound in Malaysia.

BACK TO BASICS

MAMMALS

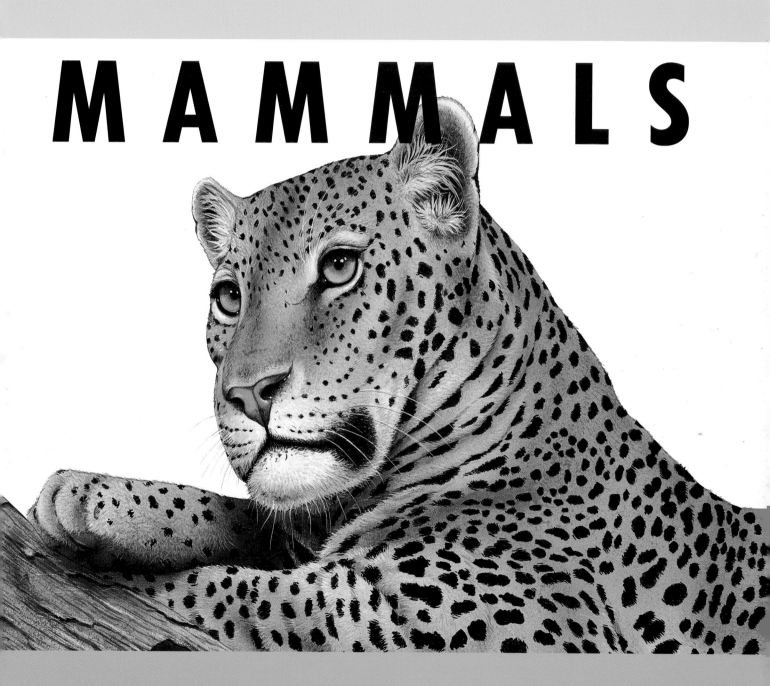

McRae Books

✳ **Aardvarks**
see page 16

✳ **Rodents**
see page 18–19

Mammals

Echidna

Egg-layers

Koala
bear

Marsupials

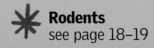

Antelope

Placentals

Mammal Groups

Scientists divide mammals into groups according to how their young develop. There are three groups: egg-laying mammals; marsupials, that are nursed in pouches on their mothers' bodies; and placentals, which grow inside their mothers' bodies and are nourished by an organ called the placenta. Most mammals are placental mammals. Mammals can also be divided into groups based on what they eat. There are plant eaters, meat eaters, and omnivores, which eat both plants and meat.

Rabbit

Plant Eaters
eat grass, leaves, fruit, seeds, nuts, etc.

Spotted Linsang

Meat Eaters
eat insects, fish, birds, other mammals, etc.

Omnivores
eat both plants and animals

Skunk

Monkeys see page 27

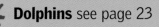
Dolphins see page 23

Contents

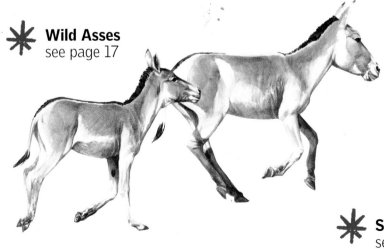
Wild Asses see page 17

Survival see page 30

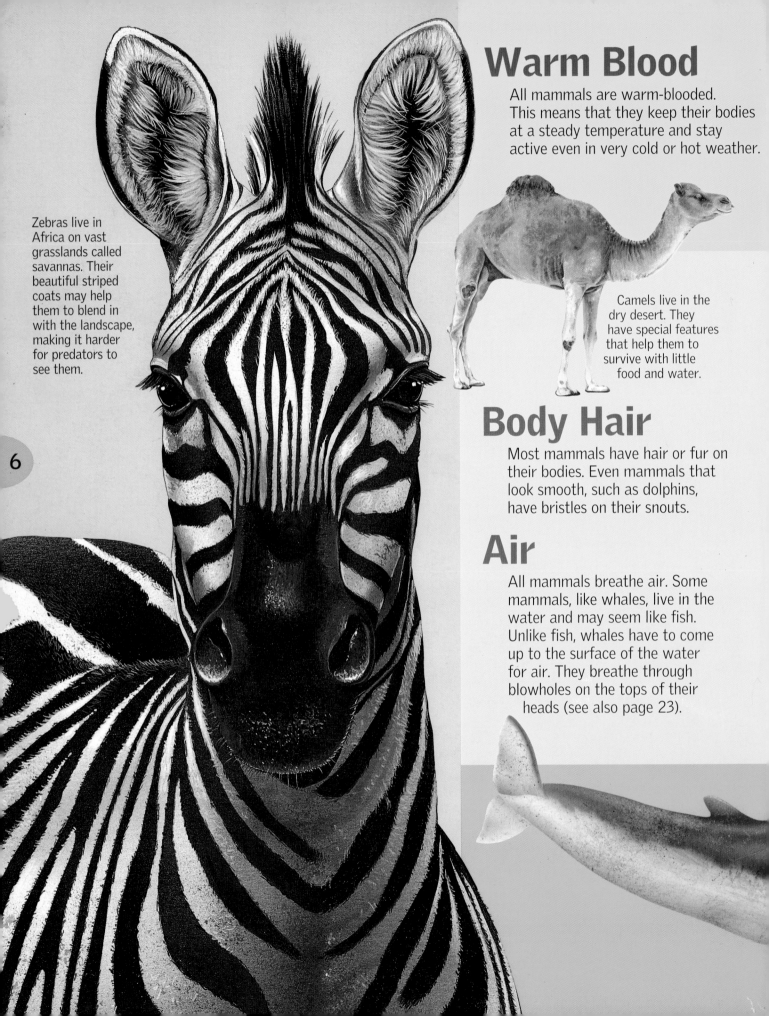

Zebras live in Africa on vast grasslands called savannas. Their beautiful striped coats may help them to blend in with the landscape, making it harder for predators to see them.

Warm Blood

All mammals are warm-blooded. This means that they keep their bodies at a steady temperature and stay active even in very cold or hot weather.

Camels live in the dry desert. They have special features that help them to survive with little food and water.

Body Hair

Most mammals have hair or fur on their bodies. Even mammals that look smooth, such as dolphins, have bristles on their snouts.

Air

All mammals breathe air. Some mammals, like whales, live in the water and may seem like fish. Unlike fish, whales have to come up to the surface of the water for air. They breathe through blowholes on the tops of their heads (see also page 23).

This harp seal pup was born on the cold Arctic ice. It is getting its fill of nice warm milk from its mother.

Milk

All mammal mothers suckle their young on milk, which provides all the nutrients the babies need until they can feed themselves. All female mammals have mammary glands, which produce milk. The name "mammal" comes from this special characteristic.

✳ **Sea Mammals** see pages 22–23

✳ **Flying Mammals** see pages 24–25

What is a Mammal?

Mammals come in many different shapes and sizes, from tiny bats to huge whales. But all mammals share some basic features, such as feeding their young on milk and having a warm body temperature. Today, there are about 4,500 species, and they live in every part of the world. Many mammals are in danger of becoming extinct, but others, including human beings, are numerous and successful.

Bats are the only mammals that can fly.

Intelligence

Almost all of the most intelligent creatures on earth today are mammals. Many have highly developed brains and they are able to use tools and communicate with each other.

7

The blue whale is the largest mammal. It can grow up to 100 feet (30 meters) long. That is almost as long as a tennis court!

Social Life

Many mammals live together in groups. These groups are often well organized so that each animal has a special place and is expected to behave in certain ways. They help each other to survive.

The small-toothed palm civet spends most of the time looking for food. It searches for fruit, digs for worms, and dives for fish and frogs.

Many mammals, like this mother cheetah and her cub, groom each other. This helps to form strong bonds between individuals and within groups.

At Work

8

Many plant-eating mammals spend almost all their time searching for leaves, grass, flowers, fruits, nuts, and other vegetation. Some meat eaters are skillful hunters. They may spend a lot of time tracking their prey but when they catch something they have a big meal often followed by a long rest.

Caring

Most mammal parents look after their young for some time after they are born. They teach them which are the best foods to eat and how to find or catch them. Mammal parents also show their young how to avoid being eaten by predators.

Play fighting can look ferocious, but nobody gets hurt.

At Play

Some baby mammals, including wolves, lions, and bears, play with their brothers and sisters. Play fighting teaches them social skills and also helps them to improve their coordination and strength.

Everyday Life
of Mammals

Some mammals have easier lives than others. Many spend most of their time looking for food and trying to keep safe from predators. But other activities, like finding a mate and caring for offspring, are also vital for survival. Almost all mammals give birth to tiny, helpless young. Their parents protect them and teach them how to survive.

The male yellow-handed titi, a kind of monkey, chooses only one mate for life. The males spend most of their time caring for their young.

Mating

All mammals have the instinct (an in-born force which causes certain behavior) to produce young. Male mammals usually have to fight other males to win over females. Others have to work hard to attract females by making loud calls, showing off, or by producing special scents.

Lions live in family groups, called prides, headed by a male. The lionesses take good care of their own young, as well as the cubs of other lionesses.

Egg-Layers

The egg-layers are the oldest type of mammal. Only three kinds of egg-laying mammals still exist: the platypus and two kinds of echidna (also known as spiny anteaters). They all live in Australia and New Guinea.

When the baby platypuses are born, the entrance to the burrow is closed up with leaves and grass. The mother leaves the burrow to look for food using an underwater entrance which most predators can not reach.

Sticky Eggs

After mating, the female echidna lays a single sticky, rubbery-skinned egg into a small pouch on her belly. The baby echidna stays inside the pouch after it hatches and is fed on milk.

Platypus Dens

The duck-billed platypus has webbed feet and a strong flat tail which are perfectly suited to its waterside lifestyle. When it is time, the female digs a burrow where she lays her eggs. The baby platypuses stay safe in the burrow for three to four months.

Wombats (right) are marsupials. They take care of their young in deep underground burrows.

Ouch! At two to three months baby echidnas develop their sharp spines. That is when they leave their mother's pouches.

Inside the Pouch

Baby kangaroos, called joeys, are not developed enough to live in the outside world when they are born. They climb up into their mothers' pouch where they feed until they are big enough to come out.

A joey suckles milk inside its mother's pouch.

Eggs
and Pouches

Marsupial mammals spend the first part of their lives inside a pouch on their mothers' stomachs. A very small group of mammals, called monotremes, lays soft-shelled eggs which hatch after about 10 days.

Marsupials

There are about 250 species of marsupial mammals. The majority live in Australasia and South America, but a few also live in Central and North America.

Koalas live in Australia. They spend most of their time in the tree tops where they feed on the shoots and leaves of the eucalyptus.

The pouch on the mother kangaroo's body stretches to accommodate the joey as it grows. Joeys come out of the pouch for the first time after a few weeks and leave if for good at six to ten months.

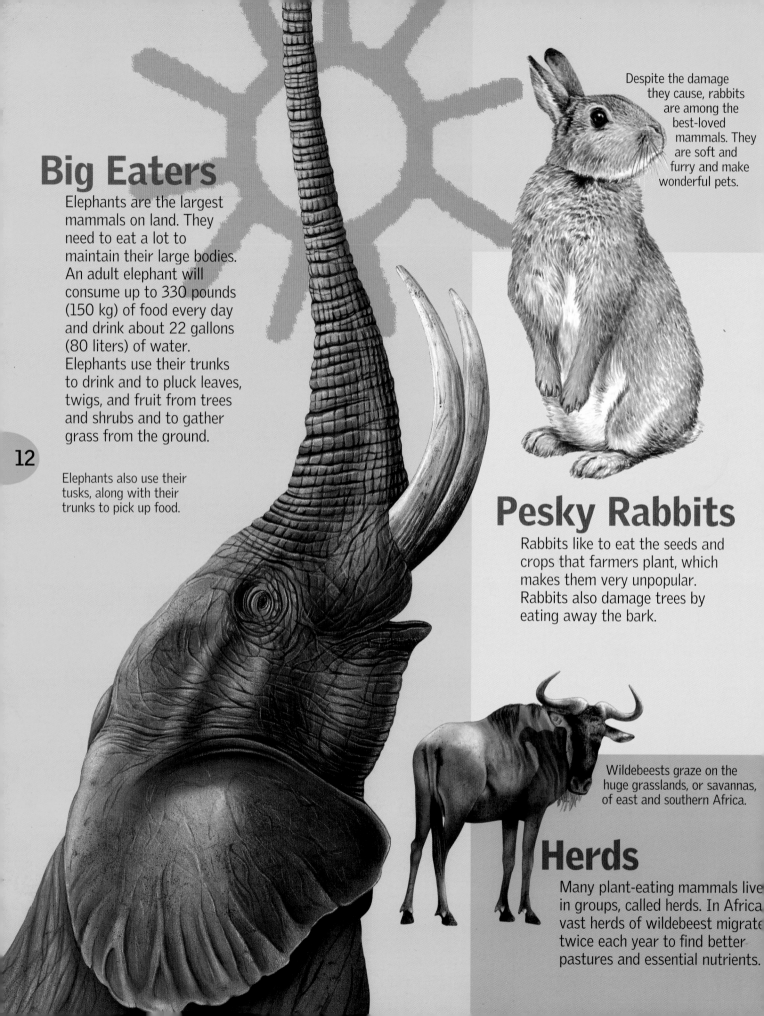

Big Eaters

Elephants are the largest mammals on land. They need to eat a lot to maintain their large bodies. An adult elephant will consume up to 330 pounds (150 kg) of food every day and drink about 22 gallons (80 liters) of water. Elephants use their trunks to drink and to pluck leaves, twigs, and fruit from trees and shrubs and to gather grass from the ground.

12

Elephants also use their tusks, along with their trunks to pick up food.

Despite the damage they cause, rabbits are among the best-loved mammals. They are soft and furry and make wonderful pets.

Pesky Rabbits

Rabbits like to eat the seeds and crops that farmers plant, which makes them very unpopular. Rabbits also damage trees by eating away the bark.

Wildebeests graze on the huge grasslands, or savannas, of east and southern Africa.

Herds

Many plant-eating mammals live in groups, called herds. In Africa vast herds of wildebeest migrate twice each year to find better pastures and essential nutrients.

Easy Food

Dikdiks are dwarf antelopes from Africa. They stand about 15 inches (36 cm) tall at the shoulder and weigh about 2 pounds (4 kg). These tiny antelopes feed on easy-to-digest tender young grass and leaves, as well as fruit and fallen leaves.

Dikdiks like to eat at night and they do not need to drink.

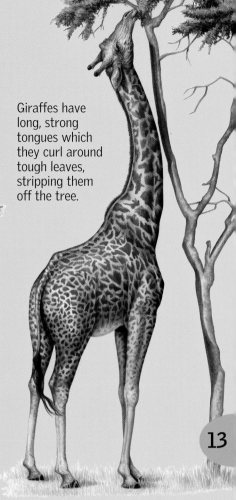

Giraffes have long, strong tongues which they curl around tough leaves, stripping them off the tree.

Plant Eaters

Most mammals eat plants. They are called herbivores. Plant food is not very nutritious and it can be hard to digest, so these mammals often have to eat large amounts of it to survive. Many have strong teeth which they use to grind tough leaves in their mouths, moving their jaws up and down and side to side. Others have special stomachs with bacteria which help to make the plant food easier to digest.

13

Long Necks

Giraffes feed on the top leaves of tall trees. Their long necks allow them to graze on food that no other animals can reach. Giraffes are large animals and they need a lot of food. They nibble and browse all day long.

Desert Make-Do

Onagers usually eat grass, but when it is scarce they will also eat bark, leaves, buds, fruits, and roots.

Onagers are wild asses that live in Tibet, India, and Iran. These areas are often very dry and plant food is scarce and not very nutritious. The asses survive because they have hard-working stomachs that can break down and digest the tough fibers in their food. They also spend up to 80 percent of their time eating!

Weasels

Weasels (right) are the smallest carnivores. They eat mice, rats, moles, birds, birds' eggs, and rabbits.

Scavengers

Scavengers, such as hyenas (below), are carnivores that eat the flesh of animals that are already dead. They are not fussy eaters and will eat every part of an animal, including bones, horns, and hooves. When they find a carcass hyenas gorge on large amounts of meat.

Lean and Mean

All members of the cat family, which includes tigers, lions, leopards, and domestic cats too, are superb hunters. They have keen eyesight and hearing, and strong supple bodies with sharp claws and teeth. They are such good hunters that they hardly ever eat anything else but meat.

The European wildcat (above) is about the size of a domestic cat. It feeds on rodents, birds, and small reptiles.

Female Hunters

Lions live together in groups called prides. They are active hunters, although it is usually the females who do the hunting. Often working together in groups, the lionesses can catch large prey. But lions also feed on insects and small animals that they catch by themselves. When no prey is available lions will eat carrion (dead meat).

Lionesses will often single out a baby, or an old or sick animal, which cannot run very fast. They separate it from the herd and then close in for the kill.

Meat Eaters

Animals that feed mainly on meat are called carnivores. Many mammals are carnivores. Some carnivorous mammals, such as tigers and lions, are powerful hunters, while others, including hyenas, prefer to feast on animals that have died or been killed by others.

The spotted linsang spends its life in the jungles of Southeast Asia. A skillful hunter, it likes to eat birds, lizards, and rodents.

Teamwork

Some hunters, like wolves, hunt in packs of six or more. Working together as a skilled team, they can bring down animals much larger and stronger than themselves. Wolves eat moose, elk, deer, sheep, goats, bison, and caribou but they also feed on small animals such as beavers, voles, and hares. In some seasons they also eat fish, berries, and carrion.

Wolves hunt when they are hungry, which is practically all the time. It takes quite a bit of meat to fill up their huge stomachs which can hold over 20 pounds (9 kg) of food.

The streaked tenerec shown here lives in Madagascar and has spines on its body.

Armored and Hungry

In Spanish, armadillo means "little armored one," which perfectly describes these animals' bony plated bodies. Armadillos eat worms, insects, snails, and spiders, as well as fruit, berries, and some plants.

The three-banded armadillo can roll itself into a ball when threatened so that only its protective shell is visible.

A Group Effort

Tenerecs go out in groups to search for earthworms. When they pick up the scent of nearby earthworms, tenerecs get excited. They make noises to let the others know they have found them.

Insects
are Tasty

Mammals that eat insects are called insectivores. This group includes shrews, moles, hedgehogs, tenerecs, and solenodons. These small mammals spend most of their time searching for food by digging through leaf litter and soft soil. Some have sharp teeth which they use to crunch hard insect shells, while others have no teeth at all. Some insect eaters also eat fruit, roots, and leaves.

Desert hedgehogs love to eat poisonous scorpions. They are clever enough to avoid being stung by their prey's tails.

By a Nose

The setting sun means mealtime for the aardvark. This African mammal comes out of its burrow, where it rests for most of the day, to feed on ants and termites. Like most insectivores, it uses its long pig-like snout to sniff its way to insect nests. With its long, clawed toes it can break open nests and dig quickly. It licks up as many insects as it can with its tongue but can also poke its snout in a termite nest and suck them up.

An aardvark approaching a termite nest.

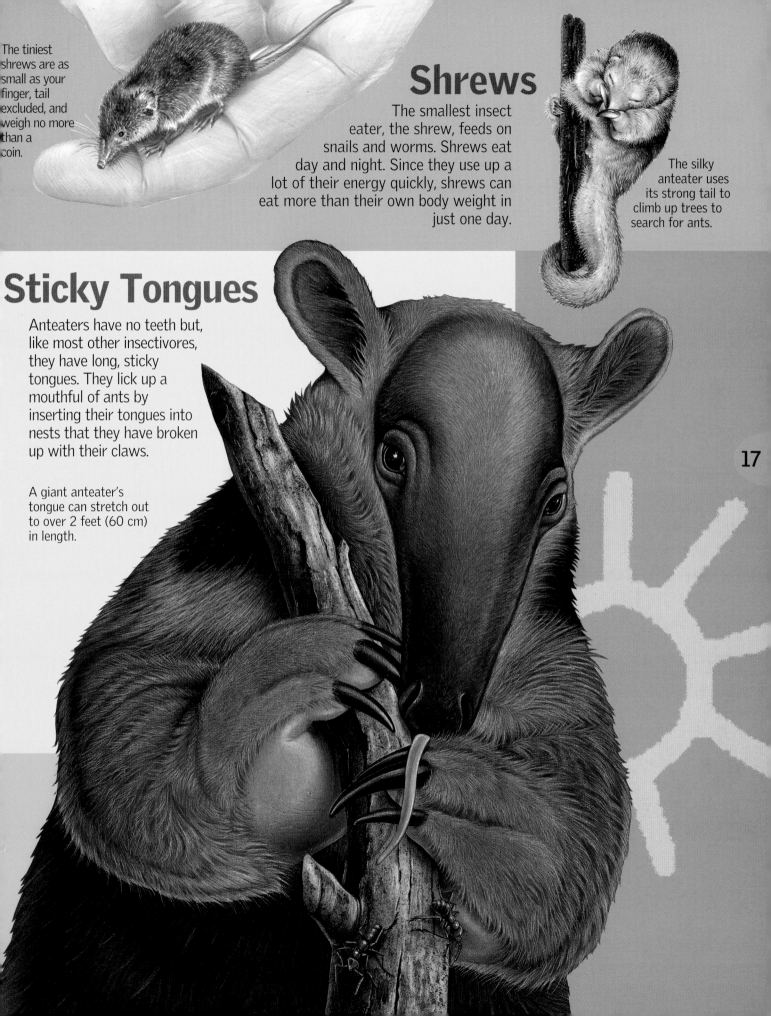

The tiniest shrews are as small as your finger, tail excluded, and weigh no more than a coin.

Shrews

The smallest insect eater, the shrew, feeds on snails and worms. Shrews eat day and night. Since they use up a lot of their energy quickly, shrews can eat more than their own body weight in just one day.

The silky anteater uses its strong tail to climb up trees to search for ants.

Sticky Tongues

Anteaters have no teeth but, like most other insectivores, they have long, sticky tongues. They lick up a mouthful of ants by inserting their tongues into nests that they have broken up with their claws.

A giant anteater's tongue can stretch out to over 2 feet (60 cm) in length.

17

Least chipmunks (left) are the smallest species of chipmunk. They live in North America.

Climbing Up

Chipmunks are good climbers, reaching treetops to nibble on acorns, seeds, fruits, and berries. But they also eat mushrooms, caterpillars, and other small insects. In desert regions they feast on cactus fruit, skillfully avoiding the sharp prickles.

Made in the Shade

African ground squirrels live in the drier parts of southern Africa. They live in burrows and feed mainly on plants, as well as a few insects. They enjoy a good dust bath, scratching sand over their bodies then shaking it off.

Nibblers
and Gnawers

Half of the mammals alive today are rodents. These small mammals have teeth tough enough to break open even the hardest nuts and seeds. Their teeth grow all the time so they need to gnaw on things every day. Many rodents are expert climbers with strong claws which they also use to pick up and grip their food.

African ground squirrels curl their tails over their backs to protect themselves from the hot sun.

Amazing Bites

Many small, furry rodents seem cute and harmless, but look out for the pocket gopher! Its giant front teeth can chew their way through just about anything. Pocket gophers eat grass and leaves but also love to sink their teeth into tubers, bulbs, and roots and they often damage the plants.

A pocket gopher hard at work.

Dormice are tiny shy rodents that only come out at night to eat.

Tuco-tucos (below) dig with their large front teeth and feed on roots, stems, and grasses.

One For the Road

The Gambian pouched rat is named for the pouches inside its cheeks. It stuffs them with food then goes off to a safe place to eat.

Seasonal Nibbles

The common dormouse changes it menu with the seasons. In spring and summer it eats flowers, pollen, and fruit. These dormice hibernate in the winter so they fatten up in the fall by feasting on nuts and seeds.

Gambian pouched rats can grow up to 35 inches (90 cm), tail included.

Foxes

Foxes forage for many different types of food. They eat birds, eggs, rodents, snakes, beetles, fish, earthworms, and fruit too, when it is available.

The red fox is always gathering food, even when it has eaten its fill. It keeps an extra stash hidden under leaves, snow, or dirt.

Brown bears eat buffalo berries, blueberries, huckleberries, cranberries, saskatoons, and crowberries.

Berry Eaters

Brown bears can hunt down large mammals, dig up small burrowing animals, feast on salmon and insects, and unearth tubers and roots, but they mainly eat berries and nuts.

Masked Bandits

Raccoons enjoy a varied diet. They eat earthworms, shellfish, snails, and fish, as well as fruit, nuts, and berries. But these little masked bandits also like to live near humans where they can scavenge in the trash and hoover up unguarded pet food.

Raccoons do not mind getting their paws wet. They fish out crayfish and frogs from streams and marshy areas.

Pigs

Pigs have a very good sense of smell, yet they will dunk their snouts into the smelliest household scraps to eat. They eat almost anything, from plants, mushrooms, roots, and grains to berries and even fish. Larger breeds of domestic pigs can weigh up to 220 pounds (100 kg).

Whatever's on the Menu

Mammals that eat both plants and meat are called omnivores. Some omnivores are skilled hunters, feasting on meat when it is plentiful. But at other times they eat fruit, fish, nuts, eggs, and many other foods too, depending on what is available. Brown bears, people, opposums, foxes, chimpanzees, pigs, and raccoons are just some examples of omnivorous mammals.

Domestic pigs, the kind you find on most farms, are related to wild boars.

The omnivorous skunk has been known to ruin lawns in its search for grubs and larvae.

Binturongs

Binturongs, also known as bearcats, live high in the tropical forests of Southeast Asia. They use their strong curling tails to move through the forest. Binturongs usually hunt at night, feeding mainly on small animals and eggs, but they also eat fruit, vegetables, and nuts.

As the tropical forests shrink, binturongs are in danger of dying out.

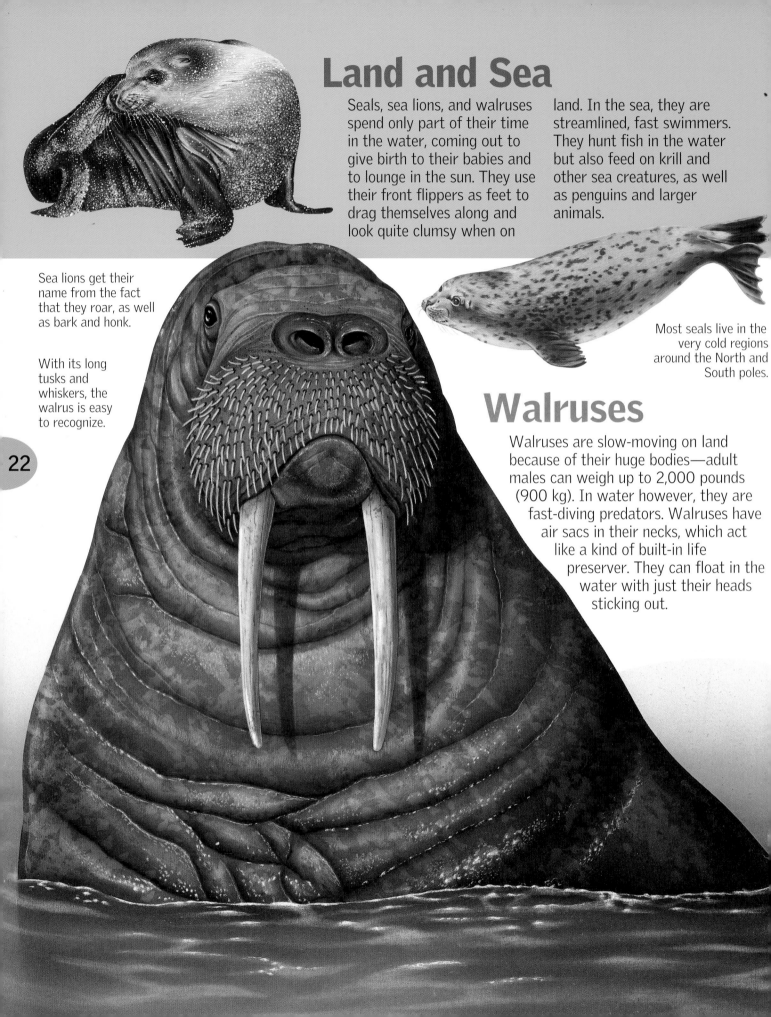

Land and Sea

Seals, sea lions, and walruses spend only part of their time in the water, coming out to give birth to their babies and to lounge in the sun. They use their front flippers as feet to drag themselves along and look quite clumsy when on land. In the sea, they are streamlined, fast swimmers. They hunt fish in the water but also feed on krill and other sea creatures, as well as penguins and larger animals.

Sea lions get their name from the fact that they roar, as well as bark and honk.

With its long tusks and whiskers, the walrus is easy to recognize.

22

Most seals live in the very cold regions around the North and South poles.

Walruses

Walruses are slow-moving on land because of their huge bodies—adult males can weigh up to 2,000 pounds (900 kg). In water however, they are fast-diving predators. Walruses have air sacs in their necks, which act like a kind of built-in life preserver. They can float in the water with just their heads sticking out.

Full-Time Swimmers

Whales and dolphins are the only mammals that spend their entire lives in the water. They have adapted so well to their watery environment that they look like large fish but because they are warm-blooded, breathe air through their lungs, and give birth to live young they are really mammals.

Dolphins are sleek and intelligent, as well as playful and friendly.

Killer whales hunt together in groups, herding their prey against the shore when they close in for the kill.

In the Water

Mammals live in almost every environment, including the water. Dolphins and whales spend all their time in the water. Other sea mammals, like seals, sea lions, and walruses come out onto land to rest and breed. Most water mammals are carnivores, eating fish, shellfish, and other sea creatures. They almost all have a thick layer of blubber, or fat, under their skins to keep them warm.

Talking and Singing

Dolphins are noisy creatures. They make whistles, clicks, and cries to stay in touch with other members of their group. Many whales make very low pitched "singing" sounds that can be heard far across the oceans.

A manatee mother with her young.

Rare Creatures

Manatees and dugongs are rare and unusual creatures. Unlike other water mammals, they are mainly herbivores. They like to eat water plants which they uproot with their powerful lips. The females give birth to one calf every other year and care for them for about 18 months. Manatees and dugongs are slow-moving and docile and they are highly endangered. They have been hunted for their meat and skins and are also being killed off by pollution of the seas.

Dugongs live in the warm waters of the Red Sea, Indian Ocean, and western Pacific Ocean.

Ruling the Roost

Most bats roost, or rest, during the day in caves, crevices, trees, or abandoned houses. Some bats live in large groups called colonies that may include over a million bats. They come out at night to feed. There are two kinds of bats, megabats and microbats. Megabats are plant eaters while microbats eat meat.

This bat has caught a frog for dinner.

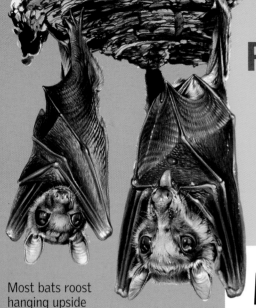

Most bats roost hanging upside down with their wings folded over their bodies to keep warm. They fight over the best spots in the roost, then settle down quietly for the whole day.

Sharp Ears

Microbats are skillful hunters. They eat insects, rodents, other bats, birds, frogs, and fish. They catch their prey using a special method called echo-location. They let out cries and are able to locate their victims by listening to the echo bouncing off the prey.

Mammals
Up and Dow

Bats are the only mammals that can truly fly, but they are not the only ones that can soar through the air. Flying squirrels are able to glide from tree to tree by stretching out flaps of skin along the sides of their bodies. Mammals can be found high in the sky as well as deep down in the ground. Many mammals, such as moles, prairie dogs, and pacas, spend a lot of their time digging underground.

A mole poking its pink snout out from a hole is a rare sight.

Holey Moley!

Moles have small eyes that are almost entirely covered in fur so they can't see very well. They feel their way around, digging tunnels to search for worms and other small animals to eat. The sensitive tiny hairs on their pink snouts help them to get a sense of their surroundings. They dig using their huge, sharp claws. They spend most of their time underground but come out sometimes to pick through piles of fallen leaves.

A flying squirrel can control the direction of flight with its flat, furry tail.

Gliders

Some mammals, such as flying squirrels, can glide through the air. Although they can not truly fly, since they have no wings, they can cover large distances. They jump from higher branches to lower branches and use the skin which stretches from their front legs to their back legs to glide through the air like kites.

Pacas (below) spend most of the day hiding out in plant-filled burrows. The entrances to their burrows are usually located among tree roots or rocks. They cover up the entrances to their burrows with leaves.

A prairie dog sticks its head out of an opening to make sure the coast is clear before coming out.

Underground Towns

Prairie dogs dig huge networks of connecting tunnels to form underground towns where thousands of these small mammals live. They organize themselves into separate sections, almost like neighborhoods, where they share food and care for their young. Even though prairie dogs have impressive, comfortable homes, they spend most of the day out and about, looking for leaves, stems, and roots to eat. By living underground prairie dogs keep safe from predators and bad weather.

Hanging Around

Monkeys are talented climbers and can swing through the trees. Most New World monkeys have long tails which they use to grip things. Some monkeys' tails are so strong that they can support their whole body weight, leaving the hands and feet free to grab food.

This spider monkey is enjoying a drink as it hangs from a branch by its tail.

The male howler monkey is the loudest land mammal in the New World. It howls each and every morning, and sometimes at night, to defend its group's territory. By howling it lets other monkeys know its group's location and size, warning them to stay away.

New World

New World monkeys are found in Central and South America. They can be distinguished from Old World monkeys by their noses, which are flatter and have nostrils that are spread further apart. They eat fruit, nuts, leaves, tree sap, and some small insects.

Northern night monkeys usually live in family groups. Grown offspring help take care of their younger brothers and sisters.

Safety in Numbers

All primates are social mammals. This means that they live together in organized groups. Monkeys are no exception. By living in groups they protect each other from predators.

Monkeying
Around

Monkeys are part of a large group of mammals called primates. This group also includes apes, human beings, bush babies, and lemurs. Primates are the most intelligent group of mammals. They can learn and adapt their behavior to suit their surroundings. Most monkeys have tails and can climb and swing from trees. Monkeys are divided into two groups: Old World monkeys and New World monkeys.

The bush baby is a type of loris. It sleeps during the day in a shared nest with other bush babies but at night, when it searches for food, it prefers to go it alone.

Prosimians

Prosimians (the word means "pre-monkeys") are small primates. They have smaller brains than other primates. They live mainly in trees and are active mostly at night. Prosimians are found in Africa, Asia, and Madagascar. They include lorises, lemurs, tarsiers, and the rare aye-aye.

Baboons are Old World monkeys. Since only one young is born at a time, it gets all its mother's attention.

Old World

The white-fronted capuchin, a New World monkey, is a smart, curious, and playful mammal. Many are trained for circus acts.

Old World monkeys are found in Africa and South and East Asia. They are larger than New World monkeys. Not all of them have tails. Some have cheek pouches in which they carry food. They eat plants, but some eat small animals too.

Baby gorillas start riding on their mothers' backs when they are about four month old.

Getting Around

Gorillas and chimpanzees spend most of their time on the ground. They move around on all fours, using the knuckles of their hands to support the front part of their bodies. Orangutans and gibbons are both at home in the trees, although orangutans move slowly through the tree tops while gibbons swing easily from branch to branch.

Gibbons are the apes most suited to life in the trees.

Leading Males

Gorillas are the biggest apes. Adult males sometimes weigh as much as 400 pounds (180 kg). Gorillas especially like to eat fruit but also fill up on leaves, herbs, and shrubs. Their dark body hair turns grey with age. Gorillas live in groups led by a dominant male, known as the silverback. Male gorillas beat their chests with their fists to scare away rivals.

Going Ape

There are two main types of ape—the gibbons, also known as lesser apes, and the great apes. The great apes include orangutans, gorillas, and chimpanzees. These apes are very closely related to human beings and the DNA of chimpanzees is almost identical to our own. Unlike monkeys, apes have no tails and their forelimbs (arms) are longer and stronger than their hindlimbs (legs).

Ape Talk

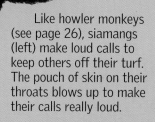

Like howler monkeys (see page 26), siamangs (left) make loud calls to keep others off their turf. The pouch of skin on their throats blows up to make their calls really loud.

Wild apes communicate with each other by making sounds, waving their hands, and with their expressive faces. Scientists have taught some chimpanzees how to talk using sign language. They can learn about 160 signs and can tell their human friends when they want to eat, drink, go out, and even tell simple stories about what happened to them.

Sticking Close Together

Apes care for their young for long periods of time. Strong bonds are formed between mother and child. But many adult male apes also help out by protecting them from danger and sharing food. Gorillas make extraordinary mammal parents. They also adopt abandoned babies, taking care of them as if they were their own.

Baby bonobos are born helpless. They are carried around by their mothers for the first two years of their lives.

Orangutans spend most of their time in the lower parts of trees. They make themselves a new sleeping nest each night before laying down to rest.

Chimpanzees have very expressive faces.

Clever Chimps

Chimpanzees are very intelligent animals, second only to human beings. They are able to express emotions, letting others know when they are happy, sad, or afraid. Chimpanzees are also able to make tools. Some use pointed sticks to scoop out termites from their nests. Bonobos, also called pygmy chimpanzees, belong to the same family as chimpanzees.

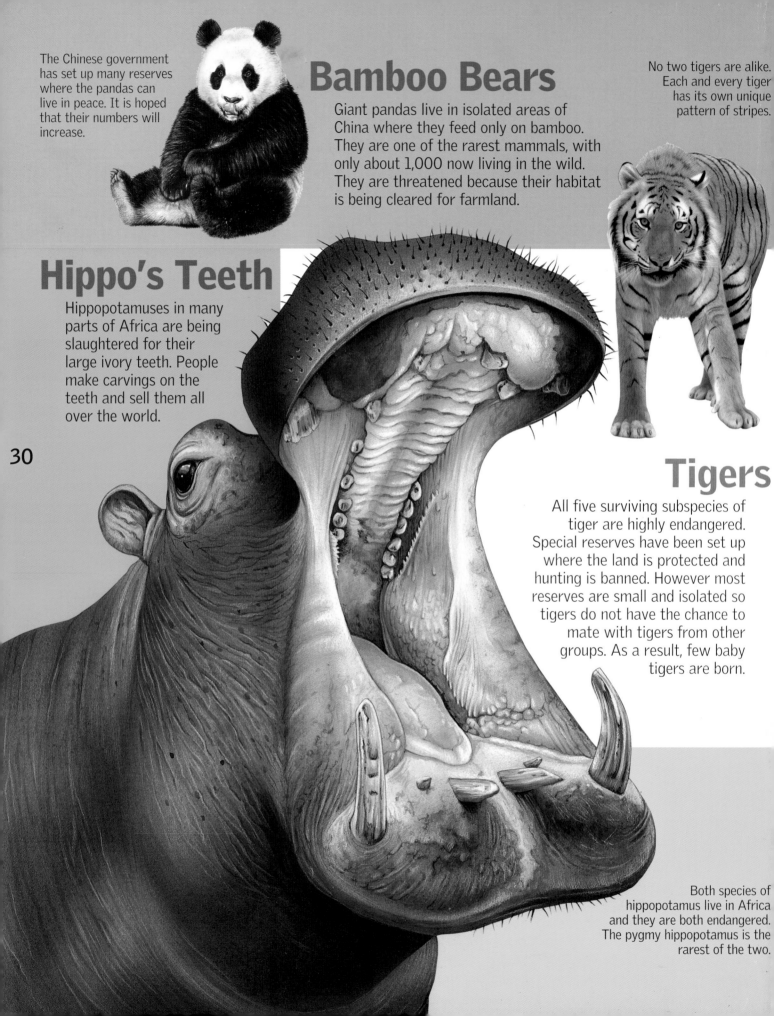

The Chinese government has set up many reserves where the pandas can live in peace. It is hoped that their numbers will increase.

Bamboo Bears

Giant pandas live in isolated areas of China where they feed only on bamboo. They are one of the rarest mammals, with only about 1,000 now living in the wild. They are threatened because their habitat is being cleared for farmland.

No two tigers are alike. Each and every tiger has its own unique pattern of stripes.

Hippo's Teeth

Hippopotamuses in many parts of Africa are being slaughtered for their large ivory teeth. People make carvings on the teeth and sell them all over the world.

Tigers

All five surviving subspecies of tiger are highly endangered. Special reserves have been set up where the land is protected and hunting is banned. However most reserves are small and isolated so tigers do not have the chance to mate with tigers from other groups. As a result, few baby tigers are born.

Both species of hippopotamus live in Africa and they are both endangered. The pygmy hippopotamus is the rarest of the two.

Cats in Trouble

Snow leopards live in the tall mountains of Central Asia. Only a few thousand remain in the wild. They are hunted for their beautiful fur and also for their bones which are used in traditional medicine. Local farmers kill them too because the leopards sometimes attack farm animals.

Unlike common leopards, snow leopards can not fully roar.

Survival

About one mammal species in four is in danger of becoming extinct. Many die out because the land they live on is cleared to make farms, or destroyed by logging and mining. Others are threatened by hunting and the sale of wild animals (or parts of their bodies). Many people all over the world are trying to save endangered mammals.

Success!

The Arabian oryx (below) became extinct in its desert homelands in the Middle East in the early 1970s. It was hunted for its meat and hide as well as for sport. But some oryx had been kept in zoos. Scientists were able to let many of them go in their old homelands. Many have survived and are now breeding again in the wild.

31

The Arabian oryx is well suited to desert life and can go for long periods without drinking.

Animals to Save

The name orangutan comes from Malay and Indonesian words that mean "man of the forest."

Orangutans used to live in rain forests all over Southeast Asia. Today they are found only in parts of Borneo and Sumatra. These shy, gentle, and very intelligent creatures are threatened because their forests are gradually being destroyed.

Index